For Shirley, Leon and Samantha.
With love. NB

For Sarahjane, Sam and James.
With love. ME

First printed 2007
by Egmont UK Limited
239 Kensington High Street, London W8 6SA

Text copyright © Nick Butterworth 2007
Illustrations copyright © Michael Evans 2007
All rights reserved
Nick Butterworth and Michael Evans have asserted their moral rights.

ISBN HB 9 7814 0521 789 7
ISBN PB 9 7814 0521 790 3

A CIP catalogue record for this title is available from The British Library
1 3 5 7 9 10 8 6 4 2
Printed in Singapore

NICK BUTTERWORTH

A Present for
Freddie Small
x x x

Illustrated by
MICHAEL EVANS

EGMONT

Freddie Small had a big problem. He didn't
like going to bed.

His mum and dad couldn't understand it. Freddie did like
his bedroom, and he loved his starry bed cover. He definitely
wasn't scared of the dark. And anyway, the landing light was
always left on. Just in case.

Freddie's mum and dad tried all sorts of things.

His mum read him long stories to help him off to sleep.

But it was Freddie's mum who ended up snoring!

His dad tried singing lullabies. But Freddie's dad
was better at keeping people awake with his singing
than getting them off to sleep.

Freddie's mum and dad wondered if it might help
if he went to bed with one of his favourite toys.
Rufus, perhaps. Or Sparky. Or Moby.

Moby, the plastic whale, was great fun at bath time.
But when Freddie put him on his pillow one night,
bath water leaked out and Moby wet the bed.

Sparky was a robot. He had flashing lights and he could
say words. Things like, "Checking Life Support Systems,"
and "Emergency!"

But Sparky's Life Support Systems were not very cuddly
to sleep next to. And one night Freddie rolled onto one
of Sparky's switches. Sparky woke everybody up shouting,
"Emergency! Emergency! EMERGENCY!"

Rufus the fox had soft fur. But one day Rufus decided
to go off on his own.

Freddie's dad tried to explain that sometimes foxes,
even toy foxes, need to go exploring. It didn't really help.
Rufus was gone. And Freddie Small still hated bedtime.

Freddie's mum and dad didn't know what to do, especially as Freddie was going to spend the night with his gran. How would she cope with his crying?

Freddie's gran was wise and clever. She had wise and clever hair and she wore wise and clever clothes.

Freddie's gran knew things. Important things like which way round batteries go and what colours make purple.

Good old Gran. She had been looking forward to Freddie's
visit. And she was ready . . .

Gran had thought of lots of things for them to do together. They played a game out in the garden. Then they made some iced buns with cherries on top.

After that, they played a dressing up game. By the time they'd finished that, the buns were ready to eat, so they had two each with a glass of milk.

They made puppets. And they made music. They made up a funny song with silly words and even sillier actions!

It was a very happy day.

And a very tiring one.

At bedtime, there were no tears.

"Come along, my sunshine," said Gran. "Let's get you washed
and into bed. Oh my! You're nearly asleep already!"

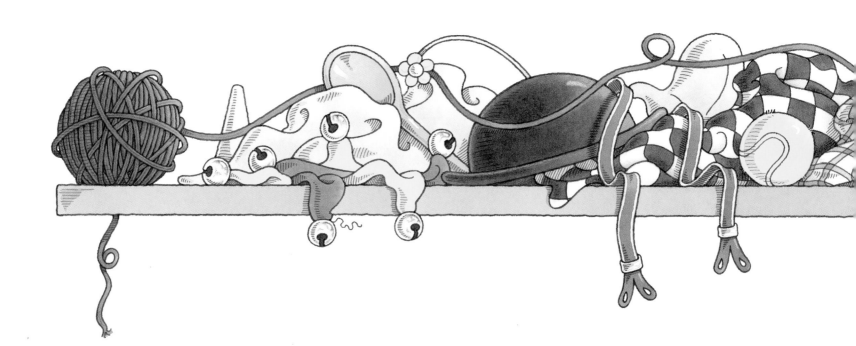

Later, when Freddie was fast asleep, Gran had an idea. She made
a big pile of all sorts of things on the kitchen table.
Then, smiling to herself and singing one of those songs
that only grans know, she got busy . . .

The next evening, Gran knocked on the door of number 49 Benhurst Avenue.

"Hello, my dears," she said to Freddie's mum and dad. "Where's that boy of ours?"

Freddie's dad didn't say anything. He didn't need to.

"WAAAAAAAAAA!" Freddie was crying again.

Gran smiled. "Don't worry," she said. "I've got just the thing."

She opened the box.

Freddie's dad jumped back in surprise. "You can't give him that!" he said.

"He'll have nightmares!" said Freddie's mum.

"Nonsense!" said Gran. "This little chap wouldn't frighten a fly!" and she went straight up the stairs towards Freddie's bedroom.

"No!" shouted Freddie's mum and dad together. At the top of the stairs, the three of them struggled with the box.

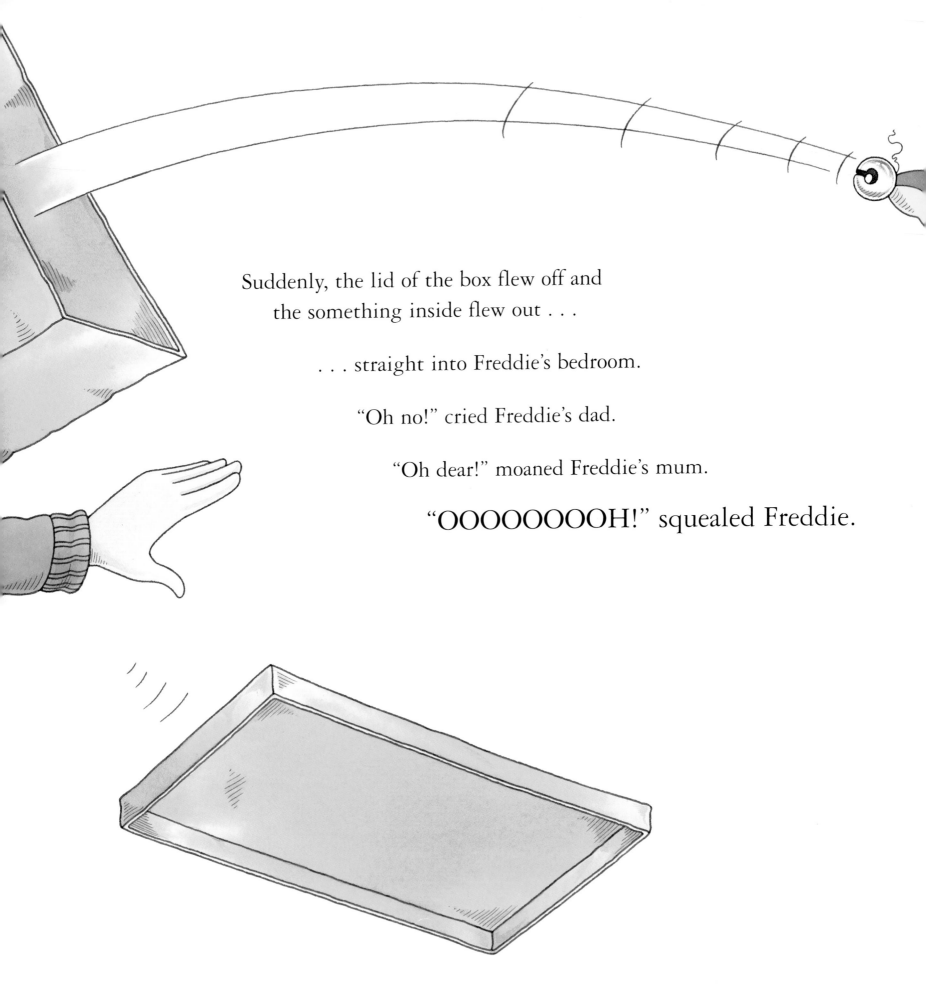

Suddenly, the lid of the box flew off and
the something inside flew out . . .

. . . straight into Freddie's bedroom.

"Oh no!" cried Freddie's dad.

"Oh dear!" moaned Freddie's mum.

"OOOOOOOOH!" squealed Freddie.

Mum, Dad and Gran all peered around the bedroom door.
Freddie was sitting up in bed hugging the strangest creature
he had ever seen.

"Is he for me?" he asked.
Mum, Dad and Gran all looked at each other.

"Er, yes," said Dad, slowly.
"Your clever Gran made him specially,"
said Mum. "He's . . . lovely, isn't he?"

"What's he made out of, Gran?" asked Freddie. He thought he had seen some of the bits and pieces before.

"Well . . . he's made out of a wonderful day," said Gran. "All he needs now, is a name."

The big smile on Freddie's face turned into a yawn. Then, with no hint of a tear, Freddie snuggled down with . . . with . . .

"Good night, Plopper," said Freddie.
And in less than two minutes, Freddie and his
new friend, Plopper, were fast asleep.

We'll Slip the Slopper and Clip the Clops!
We'll Plip the Plopper and Flip the Flops!
We'll Grip the Gropper and Trip the Trops!
And when we're done, we'll go to the shops!